TABLE OF CONTENT

Chapter seventeen- zero entitlement

Chapter eighteen- racist

Chapter nineteen- patriarchy

A LETTER TO MY DAUGHTER

Marry in haste and repent at leisure

For you cannot teach an old man new tricks

For you can take a horse to a river but you cannot force it to drink

And all promises cannot be kept

Those three little words should not define you

Oh from frying pan to fire

For you should have a strike when the iron is hot

For all, that glitter is not gold

And it is too late to cry over spilled milk

And you are back against the wall

Just know every cloud has a silver lining

And the world is not a bed of roses

For your new world know Rome was not built in a day

Always hit the road running

Kick the bucket to your failed past

Just know not all marriage ends in bliss

And remember the ball is always in your court

And don't ever sit on the fence

There is nothing like through thick and thin with your well being

And I wish you break a leg

OH MY COUNTRY

When will the snake and monkey stop eating money?

Where is your leader's conscience?

What about the promise of one dollar equals one naira?

Will we ever have a leader, not a ruler?

Is the war of which tribe and color will be in politics ever end?

When will the east north south and west unite?

When will the killing stop?

Are you less concerned because it doesn't affect you?

Will schools stop going on strike?

Can I walk freely on the road during the day or night?

When will we all stop hiding in forests, and without residential homes?

Where the people, and what are is their faith?

Will the light stop going off?

When will the government do what is right?

And why is the creator not helping?

PREGNANCY

Happy is not the world but blessed

Happy is not how I felt when I heard your heartbeat

Oh God lucky me

Happy is the minimum description of my joy

Happy can never be enough to thank you

Happiness and joy are all you have ever brought to my life

You were the reason I went through that hunger

You are the reason I found the courage to stay and love your dad

You are the reason I work hard every day

You are the reason I will never disgrace myself

You are the reason why I wake up and say one more day

Blessed is my life because I have you

Blessed and comfort I found in you

Blessed is this family because of you

Blessed is how I feel about your unique personality

Blessed is how I know you are a fighter and a warrior that is always victories

Mummy loves you and thanks for coming to us

POVERTY

The maker of visionary and future billionaires

You that deny people their privileges

And made friendly lions attack them.

You, destroyer of love and unity

You gave families songs to sing but they are all full of dirge

Poverty, cause, sorrow, and, mockery.

You gave no man choice to choose but a chance to fight for their choice

You that leave the hard worker but live with the lazy forever

You take the blame for procrastinators and are held responsible for our bad decisions

Your existence has made a lot blind and forgets their real passion

You are the reward of people who are patient and refuse to

Embrace

WINTER

During a class, I ask the student how they felt

About the winter vacation, winter get together

But one child said when winter comes spring is close

Flowers will bloom soon.

The reason we all stop behind a red light is that we know

It will turn green, right? Do you remember how many people?

Cheered and liked you? I am sure many gained strength and inspiration

From you. So don't think that it was all for nothing.

There have to be people waiting for you to get up and gather your

Strength and make a comeback, waiting for you to make yourself

Proud again including me.

TAKING A DUMP

No one in the world carries around toilet paper in case

They need to take a dump, they first take the dump

Then politely ask for some toilet paper, the surprisingly

The guy in the next cubical hands them over some of his toilet paper

From below, that is life.

You and your siblings are enemies all family

Members are enemies, five minutes together is enough to

Make you want to kill each other. But if someone else messes

With your family?

You are on the same side don't complicate things just thrown

Rock at them.

GARDENER

Just like a gardener planting it, watering it

And wishfully waiting for it, that is all

Some don't even get the chance to sprout

Some bloom later, and others bloom and immediately

Fade away.

Some are medicinal herbs, others

Are poisonous plants. Some even kill everything

Around them. Is that your fault? Just plug those out

And plant the ones you want, out of those you should cherish

For a few, the garden does not belong to the gardener

THE WORLD AGAINST YOU

When has the world ever gone the way
we want it to?

When has the world gone our way?

When have we ever wanted something
and gotten them easily

You must know how to handle things
you hate to protect

What's precious, is that someday you
will face a real sword

Not the wooden one

The world will force you that you
wouldn't be able to cry

The world will teach you how to
swallow your tears

Those tears that couldn't fall were swallowed

The world will make you wonder where they all went

And one day, you will realize because of life circumstances

And the tears you could not weep swelled like a lump

And eventually set at a place in your head

IMPORTANT OF YOUR CHOICE

All humans are faced with a choice and them all

Have consequence

Those who stomp on others don't remember

Only those who got stomped on Remember

Someone's pain might have been just a moment

To someone who inflicted it but to the victim it a

Lifetime trauma

Stop blaming others for everything and think about why

Things happened the way they did!

SUICIDE IS NOT AN OPTION

Life is like a tunnel with no end, and you

Can't escape, so...... you have decided to jump

From the roof and die?

Is that the best way? Okay, then. Die

If you feel like death is the answer. Then die

Because didn't you already decide to die on your way up?

What? Are you scared? Now that you are here?

Are you whining so someone will notice that you are having a hard time?

With time, you should forget about it. If you couldn't, you

Should have overcome it.

Do you think everything will be over if you die?

Do you think it will hurt less than it does now?

If you are right it is up to you whether you live or die. But try

To get over it. If you can't, try harder, have you ever thought of overcoming it?

They bully you because you are so weak and because

You don't have the will or bravery to fight and because

You are an easy target, your existence itself is a nuisance to everyone

Your life could be in so much pain that you might not

Have any other choice but hold on, pain is the essence of life

It is a living human fate to struggle and move forward despite that pain

MY BRAVERY DAUGHTER

Do you think you will be happy if you
avoid misery?

There is no salvation unless you save
yourself

So don't ever let anyone treat you
horribly

Thank you for hanging in there, for not
giving up

Why walk in forever in endless regret?
Listening to those Living mourn.

There is a price to pay by those who are
afraid of tomorrow than death

So why pay the price of walking in
regrets

Don’t ever let anyone push you to think of death because

You don’t want to die, you just don’t want to live that way

Failure means you should try again

Right now, you feel like you are falling behind others.

Even so, because the weather is nice. Because it cloudy

So you shouldn’t die. Start from there as you live

There will come a moment when you realize it was all for

A particular time. Suicide is a form of murder, it a brutal murder of yourself

Your life could have been in so much pain that you might not

Any other choice but hold on

ENEMY AS FRIEND

Just like that I was hurt by the words and horrified of

The stare from people around me

I needed someone to believe me or someone to talk to

But unfortunately, it was my own who betrayed me and made

Me vulnerable to people who don't know me

For days I was scared of going back home, living was like hell

But I was tired of running because I ran all my life.

I don't want to be seen or let my fear be seen

Missed the voice of my mom so bad I wished I was lying

On her lap

I remember her voice and her words as she said

Learn to let go of people that hurt you

Don't think about the hurt you feel but think about

How you want to feel. You are not worthless and you are loved

THE BEAUTY OF YOUR TALENT

Keep believing in yourself that someday the rest
Of the world is going to see you as you see yourself
Keep believing
Surround yourself with real friends who keep you grounded

You are possessed of a rare vulnerability and signal
The return of authenticity to the world, even thou
Sometimes the future seemed so far off and scary
But just keep reminding yourself that your dream is possible

A lot of people made it to the top, so can you

Sometimes somethings are easier said than done

Things will get hard as you climb and a lot easier as you adjust

Because everyone feels anxiety under pressure sometimes

But try to feel gratitude for all the doors that open up to you

WHEN LOVE IS LOST

Sometimes you feel that you would do almost

Anything for the person you love to stay by your side

And on the other hand, you realize that maybe the love

Is over and there is no hope left

The great question is, is love over, or is there something

One can still do

Thou grandma used to say, when there is life, there is hope

But in some aspects when that hope depends on the will

And emotions of another person then will work in a different way

Forcing a relationship or a situation is never good

But you don't have to give up so easily either

How do you know it is time to give up and accept that?

It over

Nothing is more exasperating than loving someone

With all your soul and feeling like they are escaping

From our lives

IN EVERYTHING GOD FIRST

In the absence of God luck is meaningless

A time always needed to be necessary is

Always wasted for if God is not the builder

Then the laborer labors in the vein

Wear humble around your shoulder

Let humility lead in your behavior

Let honesty and truth be your foundation

Flew from dishonesty and pride it will cost you, your life

Stay away from friends who mislead you

Don’t ever quit your dream for any reason do

What makes you happy?

And in all, pray and let God lead and you follow

TIME FOR PLANTING AND TIME FOR HARVEST

Just as planting a seed is not enough for it

To grow into an apple tree, speaking your wish

Is it not enough for it to truly flourish?

But if you nurture and cherish it, it will grow stronger

Don't forget some stuff are designed to impress

Your eyes and not feed you

Being in a great position should never change who you are

But should reveal who you are

Don’t be sad when your friends or people around you

Make it or progress more than you because the happiness

On their face can help you forget your problems even if is

For a moment

And remember people become successful in two ways

Luck or hard work, if you don’t have luck then work hard

ZERO ENTITLEMENT

Do you think your parents own you?

Do your think brothers and sister are indebted to you?

Do you think the family should set your life up?

Do you think the country needs to pay and fix your life?

Don't live your life like that because no one owns you

How do the orphans survive?

How does a pauper turn into a billionaire?

How does an illiterate become wise?

They hold no one for their predicament but found a way out

Learn to seize a good opportunity when you see it

Be smart and wise in all your doings

Pursue success and excellence and do everything to be

The best, be a giver and a lover of the human race

RACIST

As you live you will come across some stranger

The behavior of people around you

Nothing is wrong with you but everything is wrong

With them

You didn't ask where you want to be born

Neither did you choose your family

Be proud of your origin and identity and do everything

To protect yourself but stay away from people who try to

Bring you down

Be yourself and don’t ever change for anyone

People who criticize you and make you feel bad

About your identity, don’t entertain such people

We have only the human race and not the colored race

PATRIARCHY

Do you feel lonely and neglected?

Do you think the other children are treated better?

Do you cause the first milk you ever suck?

And the womb that gave birth to you?

No parents hate his child

Sometimes they know you are stronger

And have a weaker heart for the weak ones

No parent will see you suffer and be happy

These are your parent's secret words

We are sorry if we made you vulnerable

We are sorry if we hurt you unknowingly

We are sorry if we are not the best parent

www.ingramcontent.com/pod-product-compliance
Lightning Source LLC
LaVergne TN
LVHW020529160826
845677LV00015B/3979

* 9 7 9 8 3 6 1 9 1 8 2 1 8 *